Bookends

Also by Ian Coulls and published by Ginninderra Press
The Complete and Utter Truth About the World and Everything In It
Where the Hell Is Heaven?
Danse Macabre (Pocket Poets)
Words (Picaro Poets)
On the Road To Somewhere Else (Picaro Poets)

Ian Coulls

Bookends

Acknowledgements

I would like to express my gratitude to Stephen Matthews of Ginninderra Press, Rob Walker, Amy Yang, Stephen Davey, Anthony Priwer, Ray Clift, Gareth Saunders, Shirley Jansen, Christina Barrie, Lorna Lower, Jenny Liu and Kensington and Norwood Writers Group for their editing, advice, support, help and encouragement.

Bookends
ISBN 978 1 76041 794 9
Copyright © Ian Coulls 2019 (manager@holdenhillmedia.com.au)
Cover: Amy Yang

First published 2019 by
GINNINDERRA PRESS
PO Box 3461 Port Adelaide 5015
www.ginninderrapress.com.au

Contents

Over the Rainbow

'Mr Digby.' The doctor stood in the doorway.

The passage was like a bull-run, like a players' race leading out to the stadium. The doctor's room was small and well lit. Gabriel now began to feel the full weight of the occasion. He sat down.

'Well, Mr Digby, I'm afraid this doesn't look too good,' the doctor said. 'The symptoms of liver cancer usually don't show during the first stages and it isn't something we can treat successfully unless we find it very early. There aren't many nerves related to the liver, so it's not surprising that you felt no pain or discomfort before this. However, these recent pains on the right-hand side, your loss of appetite and the increasing lethargy have been indicators. Now the scans, the biopsy and the blood tests all show that you have fairly advanced cancer of the liver, what we call stage four. I'm afraid I can't offer you a very encouraging outlook in this situation. It's too late to consider a liver transplant because the cancer has metastasised and spread to adjacent lymph glands and organs.'

'So what are you telling me? There's no joy on the horizon?'

'I'm afraid there's not a lot of joy on the horizon.'

'Where's the horizon?'

'Well, Mr Digby, the horizon may be very close. Maybe six, at best twelve months.'

Gabriel feigned bravado. 'That's reasonably exciting.'

'Despite your situation, you still appear to be in tolerable health. There are a few forms of treatment that could create a little space for you, but I would hesitate to suggest that we can arrest the progress of the cancer now. I'm writing you a prescription for Endone. It's a commonly used painkiller and it will give you some relief when you need it. I suggest you try to maintain a healthy diet, stay away from junk food, not too much salt or sugar, and I know you'll probably think what the hell, but I suggest you avoid alcohol. Apart from its effect on your liver, alcohol and Endone don't mix well.'

'OK, well, I need some time to think. I gather that if I go for any of this other treatment, I'm still going to feel fairly crap?'

'I could answer "fairly crap", but "completely crap" is probably more accurate.'

'Great. Well, I'll get back to you.'

'Mr Digby, you don't have a lot of time before it's not worth starting.'

'OK, I've got the picture.'

Gabriel Digby walked out into the waiting room, signed a form that the receptionist offered him and paid for the consultation. Closing the door behind him, he found himself in the middle of a small group of people waiting for the lift. He fled to the staircase. The staircase was dank and poorly lit.

Gabriel walked out into the street. He was vaguely aware of the dull roar of the traffic, which was regularly punctuated by the squealing of tyres and the periodic crescendo and diminuendo of passing trucks and buses.

The swell and ebb of the traffic paralleled the throbbing in his brain. He crossed the road and took refuge in a small park. A curtain of trees sheltered him from the traffic and the rest of the world. He sat on a bench and, as the cool calm of the evening embraced him, he gradually became aware of the smell of flowers and freshly mown grass.

Some fifty metres away under a street lamp, two lovers stood kissing. Gabriel remembered kissing his first girlfriend in the park one evening. The intimacy of that fleeting moment had, at the time, seemed like a lush paradise that filled his world, but now flickered like a candle at the centre of a cold, cold universe.

*

'Morning, Gabe. You look a bit pale this morning. You OK?'

'Yeah, fine, Marie. Didn't sleep that well. Maybe I need an early night.' Gabriel shuffled into the staff lunchroom and made himself a strong coffee. He hoped the coffee would cover the smell of alcohol. Despite the doctor's advice, he had allowed himself an evening of fortified self-pity.

He made his way back to his desk and fired up his computer. Looking out the window, he saw Marie's reflection in one corner of the pane. He zeroed in on her.

Gabriel had always been interested in Marie, but had never tried to do anything about it. He had always thought her a bit out of his league. She had been to a private school and had always seemed to have class in some indefinable way that put her out of his reach.

And then there was Sally. Sally was warm, gentle and easy to get along with. She really liked him and had been there for him a number of times when he was at a loose end or needed someone. He felt he had been a bit of a bastard towards her and didn't like feeling that way, so he avoided her regularly and tried to pretend that nothing had ever happened. Every so often, though, he would have a moment of weakness and take advantage of her convenience.

At this moment, Gabriel's mind was elsewhere. He was trying to think through the cancer thing. The concept of dying didn't particularly trouble him. What overwhelmed him was the realisation that most of his current life was built around a series of mundane habits and that, given the choice of doing anything he wanted, he could not think what that might be.

Gabriel had never thought much about anything. He had always lived in the present tense. It wasn't that he enjoyed his job. It was just that there wasn't much else. It was the framework within which he wove the simple daily events and gestures that made up his life.

He knew he should quit his job and make the most of the time left to him. But what would he do if he quit? Watch television at home? Go down the pub? Wait around outside for Sally or someone at the end of the day? None of this sounded inviting, but neither did the idea of staying and working till the end.

In any case, if he walked away from everything, how would he live? He had some money in the bank. He had a little superannuation, but he hadn't, at this stage, checked if he could access it. He could use it all without concern because there was no one to inherit it.

He had no significant attachments. His father had done a runner when Gabriel was a child and his mother had raised him through a haze of self-pity, self-interest and Jack Daniels. She used to say that Jack Daniels was the man for her, and ultimately, she had loved him to death. There was an older, disapproving brother, but who cared?

'Gabriel, have you got the Goldmann file? Gabriel?' Marie had moved from the corner of his window to the corner of his desk. 'Have you got the Goldmann file? I gave it to you yesterday.'

'Do you like Coen brothers movies?' he heard himself say.

'Some are great, some are not. Why?'

'There's a Coen brothers festival at the Regal this week. Do you want to see the new one?'

It was as if Gabriel were a spectator to his own conversation. Just like that, he had come out and invited Marie to see a movie.

'Really? Are they showing *Burn after Reading*? You've probably seen it before. I have. But I wouldn't mind seeing it again.'

'Yep, I think it's on Friday night. Would you like to have dinner first?'

'Sure, sounds good. Hey, where's that Goldmann file?'

'I gave it to Foster,' he said in a state of mild disbelief. Had he really asked her out like that?

*

'G'day Don, have you got a moment? I need to talk to you about something.'

Don's desk was strewn with paper and he had been on the phone for some time. Gabriel had passed discreetly by his boss's door several times, waiting for the right moment.

'Come in, Gabe. Sit down. What's up?'

'I need to take some leave if I can, Don.'

'Leave? Jeez, Gabe, this is not a good time. We're flat out at present. Can it wait a few months?'

'I've got a problem, Don. The doctor says I've got cancer.'

'Jesus! Cancer of what? How serious?'

'Reasonably serious. Cancer of the liver. The quack says I might have six months.'

'Liver cancer? Hell, no one gets out of that alive.'

'No one gets out of life alive, Don. I was just hoping for a bit more playtime.'

'Sure Gabe, no worries, but can you just give us another week or so till I can get a replacement?'

'Yeah, that'll be OK. Thanks.'

'Gabe, I'm really sorry. If there's anything I can do, just let me know.'

'I don't suppose I can have eighteen months advance on my salary?'

*

Gabriel was standing under an awning to keep out of the rain. Marie had been discreet. She had something else to do straight away after work and so there was no walking out of the building together. Gabe knew there was only one thing more active than office minds and that was office mouths. Likewise, she hadn't given him her address. She said she would meet him outside the restaurant.

And there she was getting out of someone's car. Someone had driven her there, a man. Gabriel could not see clearly because the man was on the other side of the car. Never mind. He would just accept the evening for what it was and have a good time.

Marie had let her hair down. During the day, she had an attractive ponytail, but now her hair cascaded down around her shoulders like a waterfall, splashing playfully over her back and shoulders. She had exchanged her daytime business suit for stylish jeans and a more relaxed jacket. She saw him waiting outside the restaurant and smiled. It was a warm smile that melted away the nervousness fluttering unacknowledged inside Gabriel.

'Hi. Been here long?' she asked. 'I hope I haven't kept you waiting.'

'Just got here,' was almost the truth, but certainly a better answer. 'Let's go in.'

A waiter greeted them, checked the booking and ushered them to a table for two by the window. Outside, fine rain descended gently like a veil to an empty street that seemed to flow like a canal. On the far bank, someone would occasionally pass by, huddled under an umbrella. The streetlights cast a golden sheet over everything, interrupted here and there by scattered reds and greens that flashed from neon signs. The glass was thick, so no sound from outside penetrated to disturb the discreet but ultimately tiresome music that emanated from the ceiling speakers.

'OK, absolutely no shop talk, agreed?' he said.

She laughed, but said nothing, leaving Gabriel the decision about where the conversation might go.

'So, you've seen *Burn after Reading* before?'

'Twice, but I really like it. It's probably my favourite Coen brothers, along with *Fargo*.'

This was encouraging. The fact that she had seen the film twice before left him room to think that she had agreed to the date partly because of him.

At this point, the waiter came back with a menu and asked if they wanted something to drink. Surprisingly, Marie asked for a glass of house red. She chose a pasta dish, nothing exotic, and Gabriel felt some of his nervousness dissolve. He had dosed up on Endone before coming and decided that abstinence from alcohol was the wiser path. He asked for mineral water. The meal came.

'So what do you get into when you're not at work?' Marie asked.

'More work.'

'No, come on, really. What else do you do?' She reached across and helped herself to the salad.

'I'm studying to be a brain surgeon. I practise regularly with a knife and fork.'

Marie smiled softly.

*

The cinema was only half full and they were able to choose good seats in the centre, not too close to the screen. He sat beside her in the dark and he could hear her laugh and sometimes even breathe. From time to time, he would furtively watch the dappled light play across her classic features.

The film ended and they sat together in the half-light as people filed out, speaking to each other in the muted tones that always seem appropriate in cinemas. This was the uncharted territory of a first date and the next move was clearly Gabriel's.

'Want to go somewhere for a quiet drink, or maybe hear some music?'

'That'd be nice, but I can't. I've got a babysitter who needs to get home to her parents.'

Whoa! This was unexpected. He doubted that anyone at the office knew anything about it.

'You've got a kid?'

'Two, a boy and a girl, eleven and seven.'

'Right. So where's dad, if that's not too personal?'

'Alan left when I was pregnant with Tracy. He didn't really want either of them. He's in Canada, but we're still married. Does that bother you?'

'No, of course not. I haven't any right to be bothered. How do you feel about it?'

'Gabriel, we've been out to see a movie, OK? I don't need permission for this. It's just nice to get out sometimes and relax for a moment.'

'Sure, no problem. So whose car did you get out of when you were dropped off at the restaurant?'

'Hey, is this the Inquisition? That was the sitter's father. He dropped her off at my place, and then dropped me off at the restaurant.'

'I'm sorry, Marie,' he burbled. 'It's none of my business.'

By now they were out in front of the cinema. There was a taxi rank directly outside and three drivers watched attentively as people wandered out on to the street.

'I'd offer you a lift home if I had a car,' Gabriel apologised.

'No problem. I'm happy taking a cab,' she replied, indicating to the first driver in the rank. She reached up naturally and kissed his cheek. 'Thanks, it's been a very pleasant evening.' And she was gone.

*

It was Sunday afternoon and the doorbell rang. No one ever visited Gabriel. It would be someone peddling religion or wanting to sell something. He was taken aback to find it was his boss, Don, at the door. Don was holding a brown paper bag containing something that looked like a bottle.

'Gabe, how're you going? Hope you don't mind me dropping by. I just thought you might be able to help me drink this.' He brandished the paper bag.

'Not without some glasses, mate. You'd better come in.'

Don had never come before. Gabriel realised it must be something to do with impending death. Since there was a good chance that everyone in the room was going to die sometime, it seemed only reasonable to have a drink.

'What are we drinking, Don? Shall I bring glasses or straws?'

It was some kind of highbrow French brandy, so straws were going to be a bit lowbrow. Gabriel wasn't a brandy drinker. He didn't have balloons. He went to the kitchen and grabbed his most balloon-like wine glasses. It was mildly embarrassing that he didn't have the right glasses, but he was touched that Don had come to see him. It didn't seem to have occurred to Don that alcohol might not have been a good idea if Gabriel had liver cancer, but fortunately, Gabe hadn't taken any Endone for three or four hours. To hell with it.

'I didn't have any straws, so I thought these would be OK.'

At first, it was a little awkward, especially for Don, who was desperately trying to avoid the 'c' word or the 'd' word. However, with the passage of time and alcohol, the mood relaxed.

'So, what're you going to do, Gabe? Have you had any more thoughts?'

'I don't know, Don. I guess I'm going to quit and make the most of the time I've got left.'

'You're right. I think we all get a bit buried in the work thing. Me too. It's a miserable life if you don't have anything outside your job. Have you got a lady friend?'

'Well, matter of fact, I've been thinking about that lately, Don. I mean, like, it's all very well getting laid, but it's not the same as being close to someone special.'

'You should at least get out there and get laid, mate. I mean, what the hell? It's just not a life working your arse off and coming home to an empty house. It's the same for me, except I guess I got lucky in recent times.' Don was drunk and on a roll. 'You probably haven't noticed, but Sally and I have been close for a few months now. I really like her. I've been thinking about asking Michelle for a divorce. I mean, we've been separated for four or five years now.'

Gabriel was drunk too, but he was guarded about saying anything concerning Marie. For one thing, he knew she wouldn't be pleased, and for another thing, he didn't want to shoot his mouth off and make a fool of himself. It was all a bit too early to be making rash assumptions.

'Sally's nice,' Gabriel mumbled. 'I hope it works out well for you.'

'So you don't have any immediate plans?'

'I don't know, Don. I suppose I'd better make up my mind soon, but I'm still just trying to get a handle on it all.'

In any case, he wanted to be at the office every day until he knew how things stood with Marie.

*

Monday morning at the office was a disappointment. Marie was not there. Nor was she there on Tuesday. On Wednesday, the sun came out again. Marie had come to work.

Gabriel invited her to lunch. She said she had to buy a few things first, but that she could meet him at the Wolf and Fox Hotel at 12.30. Very discreet. They talked about the previous week's film, and Gabriel didn't want to rush things. He kept it light, but wondered if she would like to have dinner and do something on Friday night. If he had thought it out more clearly, he would probably have had a more definite suggestion. It didn't matter. She said yes.

They had not quibbled about where Friday dinner might be. This seemed to be a good sign. They went to a small, quiet Thai restaurant suggested by Marie. The food was good, but the service was slow. It didn't matter. Gabriel had dosed himself up on Endone, so he was feeling only mild discomfort. He wasn't able to eat much and drank no wine.

When they had eaten, it was too late for the few places they had thought they might go, but it didn't matter. They decided to go for a walk.

They stepped out into the street. Crossing the road, Gabriel took Marie's hand, but he didn't let go when they reached the other side. The streets were still crowded and the occasion periodically presented itself for him to put his arm around her shoulder in order to guide her through crowds.

They talked about her children and her hopes for their future. They talked about her previous relationship and a censored version of Gabriel's previous relationships. He asked her if she liked the job she was doing and if she envisaged continuing long term. She didn't

16

particularly enjoy it, but reminded him she had two children to support.

Whenever the question loomed, Gabriel steered conversation away from his own hopes and aspirations. He was aware that the evening was drawing to an end for a mother who had to go home and release a babysitter.

'Are you doing anything on the weekend?' he asked.

'Not much.'

'Would you like to do something?'

'Give me a clue.'

'Anything.' He threw caution to the wind. 'Anything to be with you. We could jump out of an aeroplane. We could climb a mountain if we can find one. We could go to a mud-wrestling match. We could try mud-wrestling ourselves…'

'How about helping me with the housework and washing the kids' clothes?'

'I think you're teasing me. I hope you're teasing me, but if you're not, the answer's OK, what time?'

She laughed again. 'How about we go and hear some live music on Sunday afternoon?'

'Great, what kind of music do you like?'

'A fairly wide variety. Surprise me.'

'Are we allowed to have dinner afterwards?'

'You'll have to ask my kids, but I think they'll let us.'

'Let me pay for the babysitter.'

'No.'

'Well, let me pay for dinner.'

'OK, but I have to go now. Babysitter and stuff. You know.'

He put his arm around her shoulder and drew her closer. She was facing him and she didn't pull away. They were very close.

He looked into her eyes and said softly, 'I like you.' He had never been less caveman, but it had never been so important not to upset someone.

'I like you too.'

She didn't pull away and he gently kissed her lips. She slipped her hand inside his jacket and he felt her nails in his ribs. She didn't draw him to her, but this was definitely more than hello. How could he have taken such a small step, and still feel like a giant?

She saw a taxi approaching. 'Babysitter. Gotta go.'

Gabriel hardly had time to wave, but Sunday was not too far away.

*

Gabriel now had Marie's phone number, so he rang her to see if she would like to hear jazz-blues at a pub on the other side of town. It would start mid-afternoon and carry on into the evening, but the pub had good food and a quiet dining room. They could hear the first two sets, have dinner, and leave.

Marie knew the band and said the singer was very good. She had still not told him exactly where she lived, so he arranged to meet her outside the hotel.

On the Sunday afternoon, Gabriel once again loaded himself up with Endone to avoid any of the discomfort that was becoming more frequent, and waited outside the pub. Marie arrived just a few minutes after him. From outside, they could faintly hear 'Somewhere over the Rainbow'.

Once inside, Gabe went to the bar to get a white wine for Marie and a lemon squash for himself. The band was popular and there was a good crowd. There were no unoccupied tables or chairs so, rather than stand at the bar, they went up the front and stood among the crowd. Marie was short and Gabriel manoeuvred her forward through the crowd.

When they reached a spot where she could see, Gabriel stood behind and put his arms around her. Standing close behind her, he could occasionally bury his face in her hair. Then he found a small gap between her shirt and her skirt and he gently rubbed the bare skin with the side of his thumb. She laughed and pulled the shirt down. He mentally kicked himself for being too adventurous.

Gabe was enjoying the music and he was enjoying holding Marie in his arms, but his mind was still churning over how the future might best unfold. She really needed to know about his illness before they found their way into the same bed. If he didn't tell her, she would feel he had taken advantage of her and she would definitely reproach him. Their relationship could very likely end at that point.

They enjoyed the first two sets and then went up to dinner on the next floor. It was quiet and the lighting was subdued. They ordered and service was prompt. There were a few moments of small talk as they ate: discussion of the band and their music. Then followed a brief pause in the conversation.

Gabriel took a deep breath and leapt in. 'Marie, I like you, I really like you. I'd like to know you so much better, but there's something I haven't told you.'

Marie was taken aback but calm, 'Tell me.'

There was no point pussyfooting around. 'Marie, I've got liver cancer. The doctor says I've got maybe six, maybe twelve months.'

Marie put her knife and fork down. Tears welled in her eyes. She said nothing, but was clearly trying to stay on top of her emotions. Finally with shaking voice she asked, 'How long have you known?'

'A couple of weeks.'

'What are you going to do?'

'I don't know.'

'Does anyone else know about it?'

'Only Don. I don't know how much longer I'll stay at work. Don told me on Friday he's got a replacement for when I want to leave.'

'Why do you stay at all?'

'Because of you.' There. He'd said it.

Marie smiled weakly. 'I don't know what to say. What do you want to happen?'

'I don't know, Marie. I've wasted so much of my life, and I'm only just starting to know you, and now there's so little time.'

'Time for what?' Every word was sticking in her throat.

'I don't know, Marie. I can't say. It's all up to you really. I've never known anyone like you before. I've never felt like this before. I want to know you so much better and there's so little time.'

'Gabriel, I'm so sorry. I don't know what to say.'

'Well, how can you? I've just told you. I understand.'

Marie looked down at her plate. 'Gabe, I can't eat this. Do you want to go for a walk?'

'Sure. Let's get out of here.'

In the street, they walked arm in arm. Marie asked him about his illness, how he felt now, what the doctor had said. She kept coming back to the big question about what hopes he had for their relationship. As they walked through the streets, the tears frequently flowed down her cheeks.

Now was the time for Gabriel to speak his mind. 'Marie, this is all new territory for me. I've never known anyone like you. You're just so different, so special, and I feel so ordinary. I never quite know what to say to you, how to tell you what I feel. You're so easy to love.'

'Gabriel, you're a good man. I really like you. I'd like to know you better. It's just that this is all so sudden.'

'Marie, I love you. And it's so common for people to say they want to spend the rest of their life with someone, but it doesn't seem fair to say that when I have so little time left.'

'Gabe, I could love you easily, but I need time to think. I have two children to consider. They depend on me, and I don't know how ready they are for a new man in their life. Can they love you too? Have you thought about that? Can you wear two children that come with the deal?'

'Yeah, I've thought about it. I can accept anything if I can find happiness with you.'

'Yes, Gabe, but they need more than acceptance. I need time to think about it.'

'Sure. I understand. You've just found out about this, and it's not the kind of thing that you can answer straight away.'

'Maybe it's best if I go home now. I just need some time to think about it all.'

'Of course. Take as long as you need but, Marie, I want to be with you. I know I haven't got a lot of time left, but I love you.'

'I've got to go.' She turned and kissed him. She had not kissed him like this before. His heart was pounding. She held him close so their bodies folded together. Then a taxi passed and she hailed it.

'Gabriel. I really could love you, but I need time to think.'

*

The next morning, Gabriel rang Don and resigned. He knew that he no longer needed to be at work to maintain contact with Marie. In any case, it would be too difficult sharing the same space with her all day and remaining discreet. Marie needed time and space to work through her own feelings and priorities.

That night, the doorbell rang. For a brief moment, Gabriel hoped it might be Marie, but he remembered she didn't have his address.

It was Sally. She hugged him warmly in the doorway and handed him a bottle of expensive cabernet sauvignon. 'Hi, Gabe. It's been too long, hasn't it? I thought it was time we caught up again.'

'What do you think we should do with this wine?' he asked with mock innocence.

'I thought we should drink it and spend some time saying hello,' Sally replied with a lot less innocence.

She reached up, gently kissed his neck, threw her coat on the sofa, and made her way to the kitchen cabinet where Gabriel kept his wine glasses. She had been here before. The wine she had bought was an older one with a cork, but she knew which drawer to go to.

She took out a corkscrew, but stopped. 'You're the gentleman. Shouldn't you be opening this?'

There was a slightly longer than normal pause and Gabriel said, 'Don told you.'

'What do you mean?'

'Don told you. You know what I mean.'

Sally knew what he meant. There was no point pretending. 'Gabe, I'm so sorry. I just thought we could maybe use some of this time to be together.'

'Sally, that's lovely. Thank you very much, but...'

'It's not just for you, Gabe. It's for me too.' She put her arms around his neck and put her head on his shoulder.

Gabriel hesitated. In his mind, it was not difficult to work through the conversations that would have led to this moment. Don and Sally were both good-hearted people, but Don would not know that Sally was here. It was clear that this could only present complications which Gabriel didn't need.

'Don't be silly, Sal. Why waste your time on a bastard like me? Less than a year and I'll be gone. You've got a decent guy who really cares for you and you risk trashing him. You're crazy.'

Gabriel knew Sally still loved him. He knew she had only moved on to Don because she could not see any future with Gabriel. And now, once again, she was his for the taking. But he knew that, for once, he couldn't be a horse's arse.

'Not even this once, like goodbye?'

He held her close, her head buried in his chest. 'Not even, Sally. You're lovely. I don't deserve a sweetie like you, and Don does. He really loves you. Don't screw it up with him. He's a good guy and you deserve to be happy.'

Sally caught her breath, but said nothing. She reached up and kissed him on the cheek, picked up her coat and left, quietly closing the door behind her.

*

On the Wednesday evening, Gabriel's mobile phone rang. It was Marie. She still didn't know where he lived. She asked if she could come to see him. It was a silly question. He raced through the shower, changed his clothes and dosed himself up with Endone.

The doorbell rang and it was Marie. She took off her coat and he saw she was dressed casually in old jeans and a flannelette shirt. Even so, she looked like she had just stepped out of a movie. Conscious of the irony, Gabriel reached for Sally's bottle from Monday night. He had forgotten that he'd taken the Endone.

'I've got a nice bottle of red wine here. Shall I open it?'

'I don't think so, Gabe. It's not what I had in mind.'

'Coffee?'

'That's not what I had in mind either.'

'What did you have in mind?'

For just a moment, Marie looked awkward. She moved closer and started to unbutton his shirt. 'Gabriel, I had you in mind, but it's been seven years since I unbuttoned a man's shirt.'

Gabriel understood her awkwardness. He pulled her closer and kissed her lips. She stopped what she was doing, closed her eyes and put her hands inside his shirt.

He continued kissing her, but with one hand helped her unbutton his shirt. 'Marie, I love you,' was all he could say.

He unbuttoned her shirt. She was wearing nothing underneath.

'Let me do the rest,' she said.

Marie was shy. She slipped out of her remaining clothes and darted under the sheet. Gabriel had been less careful shedding his clothes and was waiting for her. He gently kissed her eyes. They embraced and kissed passionately.

She drew him closer. He kissed her throat and breasts. Her face flushed. Running his hand down her belly, he felt faint ripples, telling the story of two children she had borne. He felt his passion rising.

Marie moaned and called his name. She was ready for him. Now he didn't wait. It was like coming home. Her body opened for him and welcomed him. It had been such a long time since Marie had known pleasure with a man. Her whole body convulsed in pleasure.

'Marie, I love you.'

After, he lay on his back and put his arm around Marie's shoulder so her head was on his chest. It was only then that he realised she was crying.

'What's wrong, Marie? What's wrong?'

'I love you, Gabriel.'

'Well, hey, isn't that good? Don't cry.'

'Gabe, I love you, but I can't do this.'

'How do you mean?' Gabriel's heart was in his mouth. He had an idea what 'this' might mean.

'I love you, but it won't work. It's easy to say I can love you for six months, for a year. It's not like it's forever, but I've got two children to think about, and that's long-term.'

'They can be our children. I can love them just like I love you.'

'No, you can't. I can't let you. They've already lost one father who walked out on them, and I can see they haven't really recovered from that. I can't force them to come to terms with losing another father, or an Uncle Gabriel.'

'Do they have to know about me?'

'Yes, they do, Gabe. Yes, they do. They ask me now where I'm going and I can't keep lying to them. And I'd want to be with you all the time. The truth is I want that right now. I'm just not in a situation where I can love someone part-time. I love you, but I've got other responsibilities.'

'You mean tonight is it? Hello, goodbye.'

'Gabriel, please don't put it like that. I love you.'

'But…?'

'But…full stop.'

'Never again?'

'Never again, Gabe, but I love you. I just think it's better that we end it right here now. Otherwise, it only gets more difficult.'

'Why didn't you tell me before?'

'Because tonight would have been too difficult, and I really wanted tonight to happen. I really wanted to tell you I love you.'

He put his arms around her and held her close. He wanted to make love one last time, but knew she was right. It was all too hard for both of them, and he didn't want to make her say no. They lay in each other's arms for what seemed an eternity but was still too short.

Finally, she said she had to go. She got up and Gabriel watched her get dressed, dying a little every time part of her disappeared. His heart felt like a football rising up in his throat.

Marie looked in the mirror, straightened her shirt and came to Gabriel, who was still lying in bed. 'I'll always love you, Gabriel.'

Everything had been said and tears were streaming down her cheeks. There was no point prolonging the pain. She kissed him softly, crossed the room and closed the door behind her, leaving Gabriel to wait for whatever was left of his future.

Who's Been Eating My Porridge?

Someone had been shagging Freddy's missus. He was displeased about this. There must have been something wrong with their relationship, and she couldn't or wouldn't tell him about it. He felt they could have fixed it. He knew there had been minor problems, such as his personality. Bristly, thorny, too ready to express his opinion much too bluntly, he had never been an 'easy' person. He had seen this as an asset. It left him with a small group of extremely tolerant friends, who knew him and accepted his difficult ways. He felt this was better than having fifteen hundred Facebook friends who agreed with him about the government and a variety of other causes, while neither knowing nor caring who he actually was.

However, Freddy felt it wasn't entirely his fault. Cassie was attractive and everyone liked her, but she had never been all that great in the sack and she knew it. He said it didn't matter and he loved her anyway. Freddy realised too late this had been a mistake. He should have lied and said she was great, but she'd have known he was lying.

With Cassie, it was all down to her parents and the way they had raised her. They were both ageing, conservative and very repressed. As a result, she had never managed to loosen up.

Finally, Freddy realised there was a cuckoo in the nest. The cuckoo's name was Malcolm and Freddy had learnt about it from Malcolm's wife. Seething with anger, she had phoned him and told him what was going on. He told her he was sure that if there was something significant happening, Cassie would tell him about it.

However, he started reflecting on occasions when Cassie had gone out. He became more aware of times when she said she would be back late. In the end, he had no alternative but to understand and accept this unwelcome reality. He didn't react immediately. He still hoped Cassie would broach the topic in some way and they could talk about it without bloodshed.

It would be essential not to get angry when they talked their way through it all. It was too important. Freddy was not a lukewarm sort of man. He could get fairly animated over small things, but in significant things like relationships, he would become very calm. They had shared what he thought were nineteen wonderful years, but apparently the last couple of years had not been good enough for Cassie.

One Saturday afternoon, they were sitting in the lounge room. They had just had a smoke and were very relaxed. It was an ambush.

Freddy asked her softly and calmly, 'When are you going to tell me about Malcolm?'

There was a long silence. Freddy watched and waited patiently.

Cassie looked up at the ceiling. Tears welled up in her eyes, eventually bursting free and cascading down her cheeks. 'I'm sorry, Freddy. I wanted to tell you. I've wanted to tell you for a long time. It just never seemed to be the right moment. I'm so sorry.'

'We can fix it. We just need time to talk our way through it.'

'I don't think we can, Freddy. I love him.'

'We can talk about it.'

'We can, but I've thought about this for such a long time.'

'But you've thought about it alone. We…we need to talk about it together.'

Freddy realised she had been considering separation for some time and her mind was already made up. He handled it as best he could, which wasn't well enough, because Cassie went off with Malcolm, and she didn't find out for a couple of years that her enthusiastic new lover had been lying to her. He had just been saying what he needed in order to get his end in.

Freddy always knew this, of course, but had never told her. She wouldn't have believed him, because she loved Malcolm, and Freddy had a vested interest. It would have been too obvious a thing to say about a rival.

However, he couldn't help wishing someone else had cared enough to tell him about it. Some people had friends who would have told them. And so many people seemed to have known about all this while he hadn't.

There were quite a few of Freddy and Cassie's close friends who had known about it before he did. From what Cassie told him later, she and Malcolm had gone to dinner and spent evenings with Alan and Michelle. Freddy and Alan had been friends for thirty years. Couldn't Alan have told Freddy? But Alan was also a friend of Malcolm. Alan had undoubtedly struggled with it, but, in the end, had not said what was going on. Freddy could understand this. But it left him feeling very much alone in the world.

Their neighbours had known about it, but hadn't said. Clearly, they hadn't wanted to be involved. On one side, there were Vladimir and Sasha, both in their forties and in Australia for about ten years. Along the fence line on that side were trees and bushes and excuses for not knowing. On the other side, there was another quiet, middle-aged couple, Alistair and Millicent. Too nice, Freddy understood, to say anything. Alistair claimed an invalid pension and Millie was happy with her role as a suburban housewife, so they were both usually home. They could not have failed to see Malcolm's car parked in the drive on numerous occasions when Freddy wasn't there, and Millie certainly would have talked to Sasha about it.

Some years later, Cassie came back from interstate to see her parents and old friends, and went to Freddy's place for dinner. Somewhere near the end of a second bottle of cabernet sauvignon, Freddy mentioned his musings about who had known what.

Cassie smiled. 'Ah well, you're quite right that the neighbours might not have wanted to get involved. But there was another fairly significant reason. They didn't know that I knew, but I saw them sneak past regularly when one of their partners had gone out. Vlad was bonking Millie.'

To Become a Spy

I know we all have our dreams and I'm sure we have some in common, so I have decided to share with you some of my observations and my preparation for becoming a superhero spy.

It is essential to develop a number of social skills. At the beginning of your adventures, you will always be summoned by your boss, who will explain your assignment and call in a technician to reveal the new toys concealed in your briefcase or some special vehicle at your disposal.

Before or after this, you need to engage in witty repartee with the boss's secretary, who knows all about your disgraceful reputation and behaviour, but longs to be part of it. You need to have moved on from the clumsy innuendo and double entendres of James Bond. Your mobile phone would enable you to send a photo of your genitals, but something more modern and sophisticated is needed.

You must learn to negotiate your arrival in foreign airports. Despite all the high-level secrecy of your mission, your adversaries are always waiting for you at the airport. Fortunately, these days it is easier to detect these people. In an arrival or departure lounge, where ninety per cent of those present are staring intently into their mobile phone, it is easy to spot people hiding behind a newspaper.

From the airport, it will be necessary to make that secret phone call to your local contact, but it is no longer possible in the privacy of the traditional phone booth. This is partly due to the prevalence of mobile phones and partly because the anger of modern urban life has resulted in mutilation of the majority of public telephones. The few which haven't been mutilated have been removed by the phone companies and donated to museums.

Some level of secrecy is still possible due to the mobile conversations of numerous people who speak loudly and publicly about last night's lust. Then again, with five hundred people in the same room all shouting into their phone, you too will have to shout, so your conversation may not be very private. Of course, your contact will already have a photo of your genitals, so you can probably send a quick mobile flash as ID followed by a text message.

After the airport, there will inevitably be the car chase, so if you rent a car, you will have to brush up on your driving skills. Personally, I find this terrifying, as I still drive a 1954 Morris Minor and I get scared even when I pedal at only half speed. This leaves you with the Jackie Chan technique of taking the bus and then jumping off the roof on to a passing truck. From there it is a simple matter to grab a low bridge or an overhanging traffic light and drop into a sports car driven by a gorgeous blonde who is only too willing to take you back to her hotel room.

When you finally get to your own hotel, you will need to examine your bedside phone, look behind all the pictures on the wall, check under the bed and in the toilet cistern. You will be looking for hidden microphones, cameras and peepholes. You won't want anyone watching you on the toilet or in bed with the chambermaid, who will have fallen in lust with you and come to offer midnight room service.

It is also possible that Smirch or VD5 will send their own irresistible female agent to tempt you into acts of personal intimacy which may lead to your divulging important information. While you are in the shower, she will certainly go through your pockets and discover your used condom from the afternoon's blonde.

Alternatively, another woman from Smirch may have intercepted your text message and the photo of your genitals. She will be tempted to come to you in the night and express her admiration. In the long run, it will be difficult to decide if you can trust her, but in the short sprint, you will accept her expression of admiration.

It will be extremely inconvenient that, during the night, your designated contact has been tortured and murdered. It will be of even greater concern that his phone is missing, as it still undoubtedly contains photographs of your genitals.

By now, it will be time for another car or boat chase. Here, I am blessed with more experience as I have a small tinny with a five-horsepower outboard motor and I've, at times, been out in waves as high as two metres. I wanted a bigger, more powerful boat, but I would have had difficulty towing it with my Morris Minor.

I have not at this stage mentioned hanging from an aeroplane or a helicopter. Nor have I mentioned mid-air explosions, which must not happen while you are suspended from these aircraft.

At some stage, you will undoubtedly need to fight someone. You have probably been freeze-framing your DVDs of martial arts films, where the heroes swish and thrust their weapons while making astonishing leaps, prancing like Jesus frogs across the surface of lakes and poncing poetically through the treetops in pursuit of adversaries. You will need to acquire these skills without any of the hidden wires and other trickery behind film-making.

You need to maintain a good suntan as your adventures will invariably end with you making love in a small boat in the open sea. Your colleagues will be listening with a mixture of admiration and envy over an open phone line or watching with an erection from a larger boat or a helicopter hovering overhead.

Such are the perils of daily life for a superspy. I'm thinking about trading in my Morris Minor for a sixties Ford Anglia.

Over the Fence

Our neighbour on one side was Bert, whose daughter Cindy was only six months younger than me. Bert had a 1945 Jaguar Mark IV that he used to wash on Sunday mornings. It was one of those old-time models with the outboard mudguards on the front and the big frog-eye headlights.

If Bert had paid as much attention to his daughter, he'd have known she used to jump the fence into our place. There wasn't much space between our shed and the fence, but it was all Cindy and I needed to learn a lot of things they weren't teaching at school.

Of course, my old man never knew about it. He never knew much about anything because he was always drinking with our landlord, who had been a wartime buddy and was subsequently a local barman. We became his freeby tenants when my father lost his job on the assembly line.

Emily O'Brien lived over the back fence and was two years older than I was. She was a dish. Pat, her father, had a crash repair business on the main road and drove a flashy Ford Galaxy, which he'd lovingly resurrected from a wreck that someone couldn't afford to repair. I lusted after his car and I lusted after his daughter. Unfortunately, they were both out of my reach.

Pat O'Brien had a big backyard, where he stored a number of car bodies, not complete wrecks, but damaged cars that he could rebuild and sell as a profitable sideline. As a young lad with an interest in cars, I would often spend time looking over Pat's fence and drooling. Emily was less interested in cars and consequently spent very little time in her backyard.

On one occasion, Wally, a schoolmate, came to stay for the weekend. In retrospect, I think he was more interested in friendship with Emily than with me. He had seen her at school.

'How about we jump the fence tonight and perve on her through her bedroom window?' he said.

'Wally, before you make a mess of yourself, I think you'd better come and look at this.'

I took him out to the back fence and invited him to suggest a plan of attack. It didn't take him long to realise Pat had two large German shepherds in the backyard, maybe to protect his car bodies, maybe to protect his daughter.

Since Emily was two years ahead of me at school, I didn't see her very much. Her tastes and possibilities were more mature. Older boys, especially those who had left school early and got a job, could buy their own car. In those days, having your own car was a passport to getting into a girl's pants. Consequently, I wasn't aware of her absence for some time after she went missing. It was Cindy who told me about it.

'D'you reckon Emily got more than she bargained for in the back of someone's car?' she said.

The police came and questioned the neighbours and her friends at school. I was disappointed that they didn't question me. If they had, people might have thought I had been one of her friends.

Five years later, after I also had left home, I met Emily with her three children in a supermarket. She had shacked up with one of her father's former employees. This man drove a Pontiac Parisienne.

The Price of Freedom

This story is based in Afghanistan and it is difficult to recount accurately how safely one could travel from one place to any other as control has shifted periodically between various power groups. For this reason, some fictitious place names have been used.

'You are dog shit. You are worse than a whore.'

The Muslim boys had become abusive. Latifa was an attractive young Hazara refugee from Afghanistan. She lived in Adelaide with her mother, her brother and a younger sister. As the children were all underage, they were legally required to attend a special school for new arrivals in Australia. She was an intelligent girl and quickly learned some basic English.

Latifa was mature for a fifteen-year-old, and school pleased her at first. She enjoyed the social life and the attention she was getting from the boys. Not the Afghans or the other Islamic boys, as she had quickly half-abandoned the scarf, which she wore half-mast, flamboyant, airy-fairy, Greta Garbo.

However, these boys didn't say they desperately wanted to make lust with her and she knew they didn't dare. The boys from other countries were not burdened by these concerns and swarmed around her like flies, hands in pockets, partly to look cool and casual, partly to hide their excitement. Latifa loved the attention, milked it mercilessly, encouraging them but never submitting.

The last thing on her mind was homework. She started absenting herself from school. At first, she survived on natural ability assisted by the English she spoke in the schoolyard with the other refugees. The students from some countries hung out with their compatriots and always spoke their native tongue. Others mingled across nationality, race and culture and had to use English as their common language. As a result, their English improved rapidly, although this was not necessarily reflected in the classroom.

Eventually, Latifa was no longer able to fake it in the classroom. Her results nosedived. She stayed away more often and her results spiralled into oblivion. She had been away from school for twenty-three of the first thirty-seven days that term. Her class teacher had, with the aid of a Dari-speaking interpreter, regularly contacted Latifa's mother, but with no success. Her mother was not able to control her. The school administration finally decided to act. An assistant principal and a student counsellor visited her home with a female interpreter.

The day they went, Latifa was not at school. The visitors rang the doorbell and waited. It was a long wait. The interpreter reminded them that mother didn't speak English and would probably not have the confidence to come to the door. The third time they rang, the door opened and it was Latifa. She shrieked. They saw her bolt down the passage and disappear into a side room. A door slammed.

The front door was still open, so the interpreter let herself in, calling ahead in Dari. Hearing her native tongue, Latifa's mother summoned her courage and came to greet the interpreter. The others were invited in. The girl had locked herself in her bedroom and neither her mother nor the assistant principal nor the interpreter were able to get her to come out. They gave up. Mother invited them into the living room and made tea.

When they were all finally seated, the interpreter explained, 'Latifa is only fifteen years old. Both state law and her visa require her to attend school. If she breaches the conditions of her visa, she may be sent to a holding facility while her case is considered and, in the end, she may even be sent back to Afghanistan.'

Latifa's mother wept openly. 'I know, I know. I am so ashamed, but she does not listen to anything I say. I am worried about her influence on my other children and I am afraid that we might all be sent back to Afghanistan.'

'We understand how difficult this must be for you and the school is willing to support you in any way possible, but Latifa and your other children must attend classes.'

Latifa was absent one more day and then returned to school for the next week. Then followed a period of patchy attendance and, after the next holidays, she didn't return to school. The school waited three days and the interpreter phoned home.

The matter had been resolved. Latifa's mother had discussed the problem within her immediate community and, consistent with Afghan custom but not with Australian law, had married Latifa off to Ahmad Massoud, a forty-five-year-old Hazara living in Balkh province, north Afghanistan.

Photographs had been emailed, an agreement reached and a dowry paid. Latifa was young and attractive and represented the opportunity for an Afghan to try for an Australian visa on the grounds of family reunification. Latifa's agreement or opinion on the arrangement had never been sought. Because of her lack of enthusiasm, an uncle living in Adelaide had accompanied her to Afghanistan and handed her over during the holidays.

*

In Afghanistan, Latifa's life changed dramatically. Ahmad had presented himself as a devout Muslim and so her uncle made sure that she was wearing appropriate clothing when she arrived at the airport in Kabul and transferred to Mazar-i-Sharif International Airport in Balkh Province. She was wearing a burqa, so nothing was visible to the onlooker, not even her eyes. She was totally cocooned in a small, perfumed world to which only she and her new husband would have access.

'*Salaam alaikum.*'

'*Alaikum salaam.*'

Ahmad looked older than his forty-five years. He was fat and balding with a comb-over. He could have worn a kufi or a traditional pakol if he wanted to hide his baldness. His long, grizzled beard was three-quarters grey. However, the overpowering smell of cheap cologne suggested he had made an effort.

The meeting was brief. Polite tea and the handing over of documents, some explanations about the girl, her history and her character, an assurance that she was still totally unsullied by male contact. If the uncle knew anything about Latifa's wilful personality, he didn't say. Better that Ahmad find out for himself.

The threesome separated. Ahmad had arranged a cheap, immediate marriage in Mazar-i-Sharif so that they could safely begin the drive back to Tayjand, a small village some eighty kilometres out of Mazar-i-Sharif.

The uncle also had decided to marry. In some regions where Shi'a Islam is practised, there is a form of marriage called *seigha*. If you find a woman to whom you are attracted, or by whom you are not entirely repulsed, it is possible, for an appropriate sum of money, to marry for an agreed short term. Latifa's uncle thought it would be pleasant to be married for the five days he would be in Afghanistan, but he had yet to find an attractive woman and transact the necessary details.

*

Latifa had at first looked forward to the idea of marriage as an escape from school. After all the enthusiastic attention she had received in Australia, enthusiasm to which she had not quite known how to respond, she had looked forward to culturally acceptable release from this stimulation. Now, however, the realisation that it would be with a balding, middle-aged man was a concern and her romantic ideas were collapsing.

Ahmad was not poor. He had a car, a battered old Datsun. It was a three-hour drive to Tayjand and sections of the road were through mountainous terrain. There was limited solar electricity, and all water needed to be drawn from a communal well.

Above the rattling of his car, Ahmad shouted to Latifa some of his expectations. It was only then that she learnt she would be Ahmad's third wife, the other two still very much alive and dwelling in the same house. As the newcomer, she would do the majority of the cooking and housework and look after his five children. There had been three more children, but they had died at birth. She could dress more casually at home if there were no guests. If they went out, she would need to wear the burqa. She could only go out if accompanied by her husband or the other wives.

On arrival, she was introduced to the other wives and shown around the house. It seemed that, each night, two of the wives would share a room while the other would be chosen to sleep with Ahmad. He made it clear Latifa would be the lucky lady that night. The other two seemed displeased, but not surprised.

It had been a long day and the evening was not young. Ahmad and Latifa had eaten in a roadside café and he didn't bother to ask his other wives whether they had eaten.

'Come,' he said.

Latifa was summoned early for what she had dreamed would be her first night of high passion. However, this man had not listened to the Iranian love songs of Moein.

The event lasted no more than ten minutes. Just sufficient time for functional disrobing, a hungry mouth devouring a tender throat, calloused hands palpating the breasts and, despite her dryness, forceful entry and rough thrusting into a young girl who was tense with fear, searing pain racing through the core of her body, heavy breathing, bad breath, grunting, continued thrusting, thrusting, thrusting, more grunting, a convulsion, harder, faster thrusting, quivering and a pulsating flood, diminished thrusting and minor key grunting, deflation of the invading beast, dismount.

'Good,' he grunted.

Ahmad rolled over and lay beside her, not touching, not speaking.

Latifa lay beside him like a wounded bird, panting, not from passion, but from shock, the pain now a dull throbbing. A series of convulsive sobs racked her body. Her tears burnt her eyes and flowed freely into an acrid pillow.

She had been lying immersed in her thoughts, feelings and fears for some half an hour when a rough hand grasped her shoulder and rolled her over once again.

'No, please! I'm too sore. Please, not now.'

'You are my wife.'

Latifa resisted, but he insisted. It was her conjugal duty and he was too strong for her. As he towered above her in the moonlight, she saw his comb-over had fallen to one side. She closed her eyes to the ordeal. Further blinding pain, seemingly endless. It was as if she were being sandpapered. This time she was not even aware of his orgasm. He rolled off, turned over and quickly fell asleep, leaving Latifa to her tortured body and abject hopelessness, against the background serenade of his raucous snoring.

The next morning he shook her arm. 'Get up. You must make breakfast.'

'Breakfast? What will we eat? What do I make it with? I don't know how.'

He raised his hand to hit her, but paused. 'How can a woman not know how to cook? I have paid good money to your family.' He turned to the younger of the other two wives. 'You will cook breakfast this morning. This fool doesn't know how. You must teach her.'

The woman curled her lip and Latifa saw the resentment in her eyes.

Ahmad turned back to Latifa. 'Watch Meena and listen to what she says. You cannot be a wife and not know how to cook. While we eat, you can wash our clothes.'

Latifa endured another three nights of torture before being sent to sleep in the other bedroom with Ahmad's first wife. From this room, she could hear everything through the wall. She realised the other two women had heard her ordeal on the previous nights. And when, after two nights, the second wife was replaced by the first, Latifa knew he approached all his wives with the same vigour and lack of sensitivity.

Then her turn came again. She had only partly recovered from the previous mauling. It was just as bad this time, although the shock was not as great. Emotionally, she had steeled herself for the occasion. It was, however, just as repugnant.

After three weeks of nightmare, Latifa had suffered enough. She waited till one morning when the other wives went out with Ahmad to provide for the household. The second wife took two empty buckets, in which she would bring back water from the well. This task would normally have fallen to Latifa, but she had already shown she couldn't carry two buckets of water. She had been left in the house to sweep the floors, peel some potatoes and mind the children.

This was her opportunity. Before leaving Australia, she had made a series of Internet searches and had a phone number for the Australian ambassador to Afghanistan. However, she had not completely understood. Due to the political unrest, the Australian embassy in Kabul had no fixed address, and initial contact needed to be made through an Australian phone number in Canberra.

She had hidden her mobile phone in her suitcase among her spare clothes. Disaster: no mobile signal. No one had told her that an Australian sim card would be useless in Afghanistan. Panic. She thought there might be better signal outside the house. She opened the door cautiously and peered outside. No one. Latifa held her phone as far as she could outside the door. Still no signal. Desperation.

Her heart pounding, she ventured outside to try the number. Dead. Still no signal. She didn't realise the number was Australian. She was trying to make an international call and didn't have roaming on her phone. Latifa stepped to the middle of the street. Curtains stirred in a number of neighbouring houses. She had been seen. Too late, Latifa realised. She had not thought to put on her burqa.

The neighbours were no longer hiding behind their curtains. It was now show time and they were well placed to see. Latifa ran back inside the house, but it was too late. A battered pickup truck pulled up outside and half a dozen men came hammering at the door.

*

'Enter.'

The two soldiers marched her in and Justice Khadem immediately dismissed them. Latifa stood before him, completely clothed, yet feeling absolutely naked, vulnerable, at this man's mercy. He was writing something at his desk and didn't look up. The tension was unbearable and he knew it. Latifa's heart was pumping furiously, but she could hardly breathe. Her hands were shaking, so she clasped them in front of her. The judge continued writing.

Finally, Justice Khadem looked up but said nothing. He stood up and came around from behind his desk. Still he said nothing. His eyes were piercing. The judge walked around behind her and stopped. Latifa didn't dare turn around. He must have been close. She could hear his breathing. Now her knees were shaking.

Khadem reappeared and stood just in front of her. 'You are the third wife of Ahmad Massoud.'

'Yes, sir.'

'Be quiet, woman! Who asked you?'

Latifa was unable to control herself. She could feel a trail of urine trickling down one leg.

'You were unaccompanied in the street and your mobile shows you have been trying to contact a Western embassy. What kind of woman does this?'

'Sir, I –' Her protestation was cut short by a resounding slap. Her right ear was now hot and pulsing.

'Let's see what kind of woman does this.' He reached forward and removed the scarf that the soldiers had ordered her to put on before they left Ahmad's house.

She raised her hands to cover herself and received another stinging slap on the same ear.

'So, are you going to disobey a judge as well?'

Latifa said nothing.

He advanced on her threateningly. 'Answer me, woman!' He paused. 'Now, you see, you are upset. How can I question you when you are upset?' He stroked her cheek and her pulsating ear.

Latifa floundered. What was the correct answer to this? She said nothing.

Once again, he walked behind her and briefly massaged her neck and shoulders. 'You see, you are all tense. You must relax. I am not a demon, you know.'

Then his hands slipped down to her waist and then to her hips. 'You are trembling. Are you afraid of me?'

'No, sir.'

'You must trust me. I am here to help you.'

'Yes, sir.'

From her hip, one hand slipped around the front and he pulled Latifa back against him. She could feel his excitement.

'You must relax and we will see what we can do to help you.'

Fifteen minutes later and the judge had helped himself to Ahmad Massoud's wife, but had not helped Latifa at all. Once again, there had been no prelude and it had been quick and brutal. This was not love as Latifa had dreamed. In songs and films, love was sometimes warm and gentle, sometimes hot and passionate. This was all so different from her dreams alone at home.

There was a knock at the door.

'No, wait. Not now. Come back later.'

Too late. The judge leapt up and adjusted his clothing. Latifa was still lying on the sofa, half-clad, her hair cascading to the floor and her clothing up around her waist. Khadem showed no sign of embarrassment.

'I told you to wait, soldier. Are you a fool?'

'No, sir. The office said you needed assistance.'

Latifa, mortified, sat up and tried to cover herself.

'I need to deal with this matter, but the prisoner must be guarded. Can I rely on you to take care of her?'

'Of course, sir.'

Halfway to the door, the judge turned for a moment. 'Neither of you are to leave this room. I will be gone for maybe an hour. Take good care of her, do you understand?' He winked at the soldier. 'I'm sure you know what to do.'

Justice Khadem stopped briefly in front of a mirror next to the door and checked his clothing. He was sweating profusely and his knees were shaking. He stepped outside and was relieved to see no one was there. If anyone else were to find out what had happened, he would be disgraced and executed. He headed downstairs to the administration offices.

Ahmad was sitting anxiously in the front office. He stood as the judge entered. 'Justice Khadem, Justice Khadem, when can I have my wife back? I know she has been a bad wife. She has been disobedient and disrespectful. She has broken the law and must be punished. She must be beaten. But you must give her back to me. I have paid a dowry.'

'We shall see. The matter has not been decided yet. You must be patient. Wait here.'

Ahmad dared not argue or press the point.

The judge went through to an interior office. Ten minutes later, he came out again. 'Come with me. We will speak with your wife.'

Ahmad followed obediently.

Outside the administration office, Khadem barked a brief command and four soldiers joined them. They went up the stairs to the judge's office.

*

It had been twenty minutes since Justice Khadem left. The door burst open. The judge surged in, accompanied by Ahmad and the four soldiers. Latifa was once again half-clad on the sofa, but this time beneath her guardian.

The judge turned to the first soldier to enter, 'In the name of the Prophet, captain, what do you make of this?'

'Sir, this is disgraceful. It is a crime against morality.'

The guard leapt up from the sofa and stood rigidly at attention, revealing to everyone his enthusiasm for Latifa. 'No, sir, I am just doing as you said. I am taking care of the woman.'

'We can see what you were doing, soldier. But this was clearly not what I meant by taking care of her. How dare you insinuate I meant anything else!'

'But sir –'

'Silence!'

Latifa knew she was in even deeper trouble. The soldier knew he was dead. His ashen face revealed the terror that masked his fury.

Justice Khadem turned to Latifa and continued. 'You are the wife of this man, Ahmad Massoud. This is adultery. It is a crime against Allah, the Prophet, and public morality. The penalty for this is execution.'

'But, sir,' interrupted Ahmad, 'my money. I have paid a dowry for this woman.'

'That is your problem. You have married a woman of low virtue. You can reclaim your dowry from her parents.'

'But, sir –'

'Silence!' the judge thundered. 'You dare oppose the law of Allah? Four witnesses are required to prove adultery. These four soldiers saw what was happening. You and I both saw what was happening. I am a judge. The case has been tried. The woman has disgraced you. She and the soldier must both be publicly hanged.'

Ahmad tried to cut his losses. 'Sir, she must be hanged, it is true, but must I be publicly humiliated?'

Justice Khadem's tone softened. 'It is true. You are a good man. This is not your fault. The hanging will be immediate, but not public.'

'*Tashakur. Allahu akbar.* Thank you, sir. God is great. You are a good man.'

The judge was not interested in the man's praise. He turned to the soldiers. 'You hear? Captain, these two must be taken to the courtyard below and hanged immediately.'

'Yes, sir, immediately. God is great.' However, the captain hesitated for just one moment. 'Justice Khadem…?'

'Yes?'

'May we get our cameras first?'

The Way of the World

Harry lived in a world where it was fashionable to be fashionable, and he was so unfuckingfashionable. Initially, he had advanced through the ranks on ability, but his qualities were gradually superseded by more recent trends. Integrity was so passé, something you wore like a smile but which seldom ran more than skin deep.

Harry didn't want a new haircut. He hated pastel colours and safari suits and everything that came after them. He was hard to replace because he knew what he was talking about and the others didn't. They couldn't replace him, but, with all the daggers sticking out of his back, he felt like a pincushion.

Harry said what he thought and meant what he said. He didn't raise his voice and his language was measured. However, at meetings he frequently heard others suck in their breath when he pointed out truths they all should have been embracing.

His colleagues reflected their values by the car they wore and advertised their success by their suburb and the house they lived in. Their jargon was also part of their clothing. It was the song everyone else was singing. They had actions that they performed with their songs, trendy little gestures, things they did with their hands. They framed their ideas with finger quotes, packaging their thoughts for posterity.

They sang their songs long into the night and the weekend. At dinner parties on Saturday night, they would still be reciting their mantras and incantations with clever little variations they had practised before coming.

Management heaved a collective sigh of relief when Harry took a separation package and became a consultant in the private sector. It was a good move for him, they said. He hadn't really fitted in.

The Song Remains the Same

Verse 1: Father Inferior

On the road to Aylesbury, two young brothers, Silas and Percival, met a travelling priest, fat and hearty.

'Hail to thee, good priest. Where are you going?'

'I am on my way to Aylesbury to hear confession and give absolution.'

'We too are on our way to Aylesbury. May we share your journey?'

And so it was that they spent the night sharing their food and drinking the priest's ale by the campfire in the forest.

'And what is your calling in life, gentlemen?'

'We are general farm hands in the district,' said Silas, 'but tomorrow we go to help our father castrate his oldest boar. Two years now, the boar hasn't sired a litter while another has. His siring days are done, so, nicely fattened, he'll serve us well at Father's Christmas table.'

Percival interrupted. 'Tell us, priest, do you know Margaret of Aylesbury, the daughter of pig farmer Giles Arbuthnot?'

'No, sir. I don't believe I do.'

'Come now, Priest, most of the men around here know young Margaret. As fair a maid as can be found.'

'Well now, I do remember there was a woman, a fair young maid…'

'Indeed, sir. Most men would like to know her well, but few are known to have succeeded.'

'Ah yes, I do recall one young maid. A comely lass if ever I saw.'

'And we, good sir, have had the fortune to know her better than most. Many a man has envied us.'

'Well, as it happens, you can include me as one of the fortunate fellows who have known her better.'

'Oh, I don't know there,' interrupted Percival. 'There are few men who could know her as well as I.'

'You may be wrong, good sir,' said the priest.

'Ah yes,' reflected Percival, 'I suppose your calling allows you to hear the intimate confessions of many a lass.'

'More than that, my boy. Young Margaret has shared more than her thoughts and feelings with me. She has shared first hand with me her innermost glories in the sweetest union. Just one sweet night she shared with me and many a sigh and many a groan.'

'Then you would gladly meet again and rekindle your flame of time gone by?'

'Indeed, my hearties, for in all the region, there can be no finer ornament for a fellow's manhood.'

'Well, we can help, good priest. Allow us to introduce you when we get there. We share her father, Giles Arbuthnot, and love her dearly, as only brothers can. And when you see her once again, she may well confess that you have sired her child.'

He ignored the priest's dismay and continued. 'However, we should tell you in advance that your attention was unwanted then, as it would be now, and certainly she has no wish to bear a second child.'

At this point, his brother joined the conversation. 'And it is precisely this concern which brings us here. As we told you earlier, one of our frequent tasks in life is the neutering of pigs. Now, Aylesbury folk all know you well and oft-times compare you with a pig. They feel the difference isn't great.'

Silas drew from his pouch a long knife and started sharpening it on a stone. 'They feel our experience in these matters could help protect their daughters. It will certainly serve our sister well before you come to help her raise her son.'

Percival interrupted. 'Unless, of course, you decide to leave the Church and wed our sister.'

Verse 2: Another Time, Another Place

There had been one night of desperate passion. Helen had known that Bernie was leaving France the next day. She had never known love, but neither of them had mentioned love. They had wanted each other, or at least, that was what he thought.

They had passed a long night of music and drinking and talking and laughing. The others had left, but he had stayed. They had not finished discussing the way men and women related and did not want their evening to end without reaching some algebraic conclusion.

Bernie and Helen continued drinking, talking, laughing and listening to music. Gradually the drinking and talking had slowed down and the listening had taken over.

Bernie was sitting at the end of the sofa with one leg up and the other on the floor. Helen was sitting between his legs, lounging back against his chest. He had one arm across her shoulder and was reaching down the front of her shirt. Jacques Brel started singing, '*Ne me quitte pas*' and the rest was history.

*

Helen had reconstructed her life. Or maybe he had never deconstructed it. All he knew was, she had haunted him for all these years. Bernie was aware that he had not been entirely gallant to wait twenty years to seek her out. But now, he had convinced himself it wasn't because there was no one else and nothing else happening in his life. He had hunted her down on the Internet and found she was still living in the same area of Paris.

She had advanced her career. Back then, it had been voluntary work in a local community centre while studying psychology at the Sorbonne. Helen was now an eminent psychologist with her own practice, numerous credits for research and still heavily committed to voluntary service in her community and her local church.

He could have emailed or phoned her. On the Internet, he had found her mobile number and workplace address, but still he hesitated. Was this not something better left in the past? Would he even recognise her now? There was every chance she wouldn't recognise him. In the end, he decided that a holiday in Paris would be an excellent idea.

Knowing where she worked, Bernie had caught the train out to St Cloud. He stood at the gate of her workplace car park and watched as people came out. That was certainly Helen. Her hair was now cut shorter and had turned grey, but her face was clearly recognisable and she was still as slim as she had been in her twenties.

Bernie took out his mobile and blocked his caller ID so she had no number to dial him back. He then phoned her as she approached her car. The woman was approaching a small two-door Peugeot when her phone rang.

'*Allo?* Hélène Marceau… *Allo, qui est-ce? Allo…?*

Cowardice and panic overwhelmed Bernie simultaneously. He hung up. Where would he go from here? He agonised over it for three days, but he had come to France to see her again. He couldn't back out now. Finally, he phoned again.

'*Allo*, is that you Hélène? This is Bernie, do you remember? From Clamart in the seventies.'

'Who?'

'Bernard.' He pronounced it in French. 'You remember? We were close in the seventies when we were students.'

'Oh, yes, I remember.'

This was not very committal. Bernie bumbled on. 'I'm in Paris. I thought we might catch up and remember old times.'

'Ah, yes. You should come to dinner. You can meet your daughter.'

The Fat Boy

'Hey, son, who's the fat boy there?'

'That's Kevin Anderson, Dad. He's in our class.'

'Why's he giving you the fingers?'

'Who cares? He's a creep.'

To tell the truth, I didn't know why Kevin Anderson was giving me the fingers. I hadn't seen it anyway. Maybe he was giving my father the fingers. Everyone told me my old man was a drunk. I knew that. Whose father wasn't? Maybe the fingers were directed at me. The teacher was always asking me questions and I couldn't help it if I knew the answers.

'Well, what are you going to do about it?'

My mind had already moved on. Do about what?

'He's giving you the fingers, mate. You're not going to let him get away with that, are you?'

'What do you want me to say to him?'

'Do you want to go back and fight him?' My father had already stopped the car.

'Oh, OK then.'

What else could I say? What else could I do? I was seven or eight years old and if I didn't do what my old man said, he would belt me anyway.

It wasn't pretty. The boy was taller than I was and, to put it bluntly, quite fat. I don't remember what heroic words I said to him, but he threw his arms around me and dragged me to the ground. Before I knew it, he was sitting on me and pummelling my face. There was nothing I could do. He was just too heavy.

When he had finished with me, I was allowed to return to my father. I was dishevelled and sweating, but the welcome was chilling. I didn't dare express my indignation at being sent into battle on behalf of my father. He was humiliated that I had been humiliated in hand-to-hand combat with a fat boy. I was humiliated that my father had been humiliated.

We walked home in silence.

A Change of Heart

The day came when he realised their love was just a habit. She had wanted him because she wanted a husband. Gradually, as they knew each other better, Yiqian had begun to comment on Ozzie's shortcomings, sometimes real and sometimes the product of her own biases and preferences. He felt she wanted to remodel him.

Yiqian's English was extremely limited, so Ozzie had decided not to work when in China this time. He would continue to study and improve his Chinese. Every day, he sat at home and studied.

This was not enough. He needed to get out and meet Chinese-speaking people, hear them and speak with them, sometimes in Chinese, sometimes in English. He couldn't sit in a room all day, every day and remain healthy. There needed to be something beyond that room.

On Sunday mornings, he started to go to English Corner, a common institution in urban China. Large numbers of Chinese people go to meet foreigners and practise their English. In the process, relationships and friendships are formed. Relationships are at the centre of everything in China.

When their English fell short, they valued Ozzie's ability to continue the conversation in Chinese. People sought him out, especially businessmen and students, and he was frequently surrounded by crowds of people wanting to lay claim to his time. Many asked for his QQ Internet address in order to engage him in online conversation.

All of this distressed Yiqian. It was not long before Ozzie realised she was going around trying to channel people away from him. He learned from a number of university students that she had approached and threatened them. She had told them to stay away from him, both at English Corner and on the Internet. Ozzie had noticed the absence of these people, but it was only later that he learned of her threats.

She was checking his mobile, trawling for information from his phone records, searching his computer. She had her own computer, but preferred to use his. Whenever he went online or took a phone call, she was in the room. She was phoning his acquaintances to ask if he had contacted them lately.

A number of times he had to go to China Mobile and ask them to unlock his phone because she had put in the wrong code trying to open it. Ultimately, as there was nothing to hide anyway, he took the password off his phone so she could have free access to it.

One evening, he had gone out to dinner with Yiqian and a roomful of her friends and associates. They were all high-powered businessmen and civic leaders. The food was excellent and they all regularly stood and toasted each other as a group and individually.

They would stand and raise their glasses with a series of arcane gestures that betokened ritual and respect, but to the uninitiated would have appeared meaningless and pompous. '*Gan bei!*' and it was gone. Of course they were only drinking from shot glasses, but they dispatched them with such regularity that they were quickly intoxicated.

The evening proceeded like this until all the food had been fed and the drink had been drunk. People started to go home. There remained, however, a small number who had either drunk too much or not drunk enough. Among them was a company director, who suggested they should go out to a local karaoke bar and continue their celebration.

Karaoke bars in China are sometimes places where people can meet their friends, drink and sing songs. Many young people do this because they like to sing songs. Some people do it because they like to drink.

However, karaoke bars are also a favoured haunt of businessmen who are not in a hurry to go back to work in the afternoon or home in the evening. They hire a private room and order copious quantities of food and drink. A line-up of women arrives, and the men choose those they feel might be good company. 'Good company' may merely mean someone who can light their cigarettes and share their food and drink. However, an additional sum of money can turn one of these attractive women into much more entertainment than the law permits. Or as some of the less subtle girls say, 'Give you massagy. Always have happy ending.'

Ozzie could see that Yiqian might not think this would be a happy end to the evening. He danced with her frequently to make it obvious he had a partner. The women left him alone but, between dances, one of them came to top up his beer. She leaned on his shoulder, and her breast was draped across his forearm. This situation clearly displeased Yiqian, who closed in rapidly, knocking the bottle from the girl's hand and pushing her over. The girl fortunately landed on one of the sofas, and Yiqian regaled her with a torrent of abuse in Chinese.

Staff and other guests raced in to separate the two women, and one of the other girls quickly escorted her colleague from the room. A manager appeared from nowhere, topped up everyone's glass, and all was instantly forgotten by those whose emotions had not been ruffled.

*

One evening they were having dinner with some of Yiqian's friends and colleagues. As always, there was a lot of eating and drinking, but especially lots of drinking. People would sometimes toast each other across the table, and sometimes get up and come around the table to toast each other. It was a mark of respect but, more particularly, it was an excuse to have another drink.

In the course of all this mutual respect, Ozzie saw a woman on the other side of the table. She raised her glass in toast and he returned her salute. They were in a noisy restaurant and totally unable to hear each other, but she laughed and, with her laugh, he saw her dimples.

Throughout the evening, people continued to toast each other, sometimes wishing each other well, sometimes just in acknowledgement that they were both or all plastered. However, when this woman raised her glass to him, there was always her dimpled laugh and that twinkle in her eye. He sought it out. He toasted her so he could see it again. She was different.

She came around the table and they had a brief conversation in Chinese.

'Hello. My name is May Lee. I would like to speak better English. Do you know someone who could help me?'

A friend had posted her profile on a dating site and many men had responded. Her friend's basic English had been sufficient to attract the interest of these men, but not good enough to cope with their return correspondence. Ozzie suggested she go to English Corner on Sunday mornings.

The following Sunday, she came with another colleague from work. Yiqian knew these women, so after English Corner they all went to a nearby restaurant and had lunch. During the meal, May Lee asked Ozzie if he could help her.

Ozzie was willing to help, but this aroused considerable resistance from Yiqian, who escalated her daily check of his mobile and computer. Ozzie understood it would be easier and perhaps more correct to refuse to help. However, it rankled that he was not trusted. He told himself there was no untoward relationship here. He was just helping this woman find a foreign friend and establish a relationship.

He pacified Yiqian by saying he would not teach May Lee English, but said he would help her find a boyfriend. He translated her letters for her, counselled her about the probable intentions of these men, advised her about the wisdom of her responses, and sometimes wrote letters of reply for her. He told the candidates he was an Australian male acting as an intermediary.

One by one, the candidates disappeared or were eliminated for a variety of reasons. Some were simply not compatible, some lost interest because the relationship was not advancing as fast as they had hoped and some were eliminated because they had proposed ideas she considered indiscreet or improper. One man remained, an American named Robert. Ozzie thought he seemed more patient.

*

Some weeks later, Yiqian needed to see a doctor. She came home and wanted a large sum of money for medicine and an operation. This was OK, but what was happening? She didn't know. Well, what did the doctor say? She didn't know that either. Well, OK. He gave her the money anyway. She came back with four different types of medicine and started taking it all.

Yiqian went to the bedroom and lay down for a nap. Ozzie copied what was written on the medicine bottles and boxes and made an Internet search. Some of the drugs were blacklisted in the United States as dangerous, and so the drug companies were getting rid of them in developing countries. Some of the medicines were for sexually transmitted diseases. It was clear that doctors were not going to prescribe dangerous medicines if they didn't know what she had.

Yiqian was still asleep, so he went to the central hospital. He was given a series of tests and was told to come back the next day. The result was clear. Ozzie didn't have a sexually transmitted disease but, quite possibly, Yiqian did.

The couple had talked on numerous occasions about the decline of their relationship. They talked about it again that evening, although Ozzie didn't mention his discovery. He spoke calmly and without anger, but Yiqian's manner became sarcastic and aggressive. Ozzie was calm because he knew the end was near and didn't want to be blamed for it. Nor was there any point blaming her.

As he put it to her softly, 'Look, I think we both just made a mistake, don't you?' He felt relieved when she quietly agreed.

*

The time had come. He phoned some friends in Australia, made arrangements and, paying the necessary penalties, changed the booked date on his airline ticket to the soonest day possible. He remained silent about his intentions over the next few days. There seemed to be no point in arguing. They had argued enough. He would phone her from the airport or from Australia.

On the day of his departure, Ozzie waited till she went to work, packed his few things, left his key on the kitchen table and departed. At the gate to the residential estate, he was nervous that the guards would ask why he had a suitcase. However, they were playing cards.

He was in the departure lounge at the airport when his phone rang. It was Yiqian, who had come home early and wanted to know where he was. She was too late now. He didn't need to lie.

'Yiqian, I won't be home to dinner. I won't be back at all. I'm sorry, I'm leaving you.'

There was a brief pause. 'No, Ozzie, I need you. Don't go, please, don't go.'

'I'm sorry, Yiqian. We've talked about it all before. It's too late.'

'Ozzie, please, I love you. I need you.' Her voice was a faint husk. 'Don't leave me.'

It was wrenching. His heart rose in his throat.

'I'm sorry, Yiqian,' he croaked. 'I have to go.'

As he hung up, the call for passengers to board came over the PA.

*

From Australia, Ozzie continued to help May Lee online and he came to know her well. She would ask him about his own situation and how he was coping.

May Lee's American friend Robert seemed to be a genuine person and she started writing her own simple letters to him. She still needed help translating his return letters and sought Ozzie's opinion on some issues. She needed to understand what the underlying subtext might be.

Robert was a widower and had three school-age children to support. He had a modest job in the public service and his eldest son was hoping to go to university. Robert had shared with May Lee a dream in which he came to China, galloped up to her on a handsome white charger, swept her up in his arms, and rode away into an American sunset. In Robert's world, the sun both rose and set in America. May Lee was not particularly interested in the horse, but she liked the idea of an American sunset. However, money was a problem and his letters gradually became less passionate, then perfunctory. Finally, he wrote to tell her that he had found another woman, an American, and that he was going to marry her.

May Lee was distraught. She had put all her hope and emotional energy into this relationship. Her emails to Ozzie were lengthy outpourings of naked grief. There were distressing gaps in their communication. Her letters became more philosophical, although always tinged with depression. Then they plunged once more into the depths of grief.

The Chinese spring festival was approaching and Ozzie suggested she should go somewhere for a holiday. May Lee said it would be too depressing, but Ozzie persisted. He said she should get away from it all. She then said she would go to Kunming if he came too.

He hesitated, but ultimately agreed. She had stood by Ozzie through his own times of hardship, and now that the man she loved had failed her, she was calling his name. He would meet her in Kunming.

*

May Lee met him at the airport. She was with an old schoolfriend who had a car. They drove to a hotel near the edge of the city. The friend left. Ozzie showered and they went out to dinner in a nearby café. May Lee's English was still not good enough, so most of the time they spoke Chinese.

Her friend had left them an electric bike that they could use while in Kunming. After dinner, they rode out through the neon kaleidoscope of the outbound highway, the traffic gradually becoming sparser, the noise dying away.

May Lee's arms were around his waist, and her head against his back. Her legs firmly embraced his hips and her fingers would occasionally claw his belly as a gentle reminder that she was there. Eventually, the coloured lights flashed less across their faces and there ahead on the right was a thickly wooded park.

He pulled off the road and into the park. As if designed for the occasion, the track went up a small hill and curled back toward the road. He stopped under some trees and, from their secret vantage point, they could see the cars going by beneath them. He dismounted and remounted the bike once again, but this time facing the rear. To achieve this, he gently lifted her legs and draped them over his thighs. Although nervous, she didn't resist. They were now face to face. He put his arms around her and she leaned forward into his embrace.

'I've missed you,' he said, and time seemed to stand still as they remained silent and motionless in each other's arms.

Finally, they rode back to the hotel.

Back in their hotel room there was a tension. May Lee was nervous and took a bottle of rice wine from her bag. It turned out that Ozzie had a bottle of red wine in his suitcase. They agreed that a glass or two of wine would be a good idea. A glass or two became a bottle or two well into the evening.

They talked about the way things had happened or not happened. They talked about their relationships with Yiqian and Robert. May Lee would occasionally be tearful, but Ozzie would make her laugh and all would be forgotten. By midnight, the evening had been long, any trace of tension had been drowned and May Lee had drunk and cried till she could no longer do either.

They were sitting on the sofa. She had slumped into fitful sleep on Ozzie's shoulder. Eventually, he helped her up and loaded her, fully clothed, into the bed. He left a small lamp on and, covered by the lace tablecloth, stretched out on the sofa.

*

In the morning, she sat up sluggishly and saw him making coffee. 'Where did you sleep?' she asked.

'On the sofa.'

'On the sofa? That's so uncomfortable. Why didn't you sleep in the bed with me?'

'Because if I'd slept in the bed with you, I'd have wanted you.'

There was a long pause. 'Didn't you want me?' she asked in a soft, slightly crushed voice.

'Of course, but I wouldn't want to lose our friendship.'

Another pause. 'Did you think we couldn't still be friends?'

'I wouldn't want to risk it. Would you?'

There was another long pause. 'I don't know anything much at present,' she said. 'I think I drank too much last night.'

'I know you drank too much last night. How are you feeling now?'

'Dreadful.'

'Surprise, surprise.'

Protracted silence.

Then she turned to him and asked, 'Why didn't you take my clothes off when you put me in bed?'

'For the same reason I didn't share the bed.'

'I can see why Robert didn't want me then. Even my best friend won't take advantage of me when I'm drunk.'

'If that's me you're talking about, then of course I wouldn't. Best friends don't take advantage of each other.'

'And when I'm not drunk?'

'Best friends don't take advantage of each other any time at all. Robert's crazy,' Ozzie changed the subject. 'You're gorgeous, but he was lazy and impatient. He wasn't willing to learn Chinese, and he wasn't willing to wait for you to learn English. We talked about all that last night.'

'Ozzie...'

He looked up and she was crying. He went to her, 'Hey, hey, it's OK. He was crazy. You're beautiful.'

'Why don't you want me then, Ozzie?'

'Of course I want you, May. Of course I want you.'

*

The days and weeks passed. They went places and did things. They made love regularly and were happy. More importantly, they enjoyed sharing daily life, doing all the simple things that people do.

Too soon, however, Ozzie's visa was expiring and he had to leave China. The evening before, they went out to dinner, shared a bottle of wine and went back to the hotel. In their room, he held her in his arms and she clung to him long into the night.

Early in the morning, they showered together and checked out. At the airport, they didn't dwell on farewell. It was too painful and, anyway, all had been said.

With Ozzie back in Australia, their only contact was via the Internet. Sometimes they just looked at each other. Their relationship was held together by memories and dreams. It was wrenching that they wanted each other but were separated by two computer screens. Later, they came to feel that it was just the one screen, the screen they each saw. And then their hearts reached out across the screen, across time and space, and became one.

*

There was something Ozzie hadn't told her. He was not young, and it had not been easy trying to learn Chinese. It isn't easy learning Chinese at any age, but now, as the years advanced, he was becoming aware that his mental capacities were fading. His memory was starting to fail. It was not just his Chinese. His English also was developing gaps. He was starting to stutter. He frequently couldn't remember the words he needed. People's names came and went.

He had seen his doctor several years earlier. The doctor had performed several perfunctory tests, and declared that Ozzie didn't have a problem. What did he expect at his age, the doctor had asked. However, his condition had slowly deteriorated.

Ozzie told May Lee of his fears. She tried to reassure him, but these were just the things we say to comfort people in their moments of crisis. Hey, it's OK. You didn't need that leg anyway.

Finally, she realised the problem was real, quit her job and came to him. She did so without any concern for her own financial situation, but he immediately said he would pay the Chinese pension she would have received if she had waited for correct procedure. There were agonising months going through the mind-numbing inquisition required by both countries before she was granted a tourist visa. She had no intention of respecting the three-month term of the visa.

The doctor now acknowledged that Ozzie's capabilities were diminishing. Further tests were done and Alzheimer's disease was diagnosed. Ozzie made further financial arrangements to protect and provide for May Lee, gave her power of attorney and power of decision in an advance care directive. She said she didn't care and didn't want these things, but he pointed out that the provisions were necessary for his own welfare and security as well.

Throughout this time, Ozzie was still functioning. The doctor said that, although his condition was deteriorating, they could still have some remaining time of happiness. They profited from it and travelled. Ozzie insisted May Lee avoid visa problems, so they went back to China and organised a second tourist visa.

Each night they lay together and held each other, sometimes gently, sometimes passionately. They made love and then lay talking. Each morning, they awoke beside each other and lay listening to the birdsong outside their window.

They clung passionately to the present moment, not wanting to think about the future. Gradually, May Lee realised she was losing him. At times there was a vacant stare that seemed unaware of her